# THE FLYAWAY PANTALOONS

illustrated by Sue Scullard ▪ verses by Joseph Sharples

Carolrhoda Books, Inc./Minneapolis

This edition first published 1990 by Carolrhoda Books, Inc.
Originally published by Macmillan Children's Books, London.
Illustrations copyright © 1988 by Sue Scullard.
Text copyright © 1988 by Macmillan Publishers, Ltd.
All rights to this edition reserved by Carolrhoda Books, Inc.

LIBRARY OF CONGRESS CATALOGING-IN-PUBLICATION DATA

Scullard, Sue.
The flyaway pantaloons / Sue Scullard.
p.    cm.
Summary: A pair of pantaloons relates how, after being blown off
its clothesline, it had an exciting adventure before returning where
it belonged.
ISBN 0-87614-408-3 (lib. bdg.)
[1. Clothing and dress—Fiction.   2. Stories in rhyme.]
I. Title.
PZ8.3.S4434F1   1990
[E]—dc20                                        89-37454
                                                CIP
                                                AC

Manufactured in the United States of America

1  2  3  4  5  6  7  8  9  10  00  99  98  97  96  95  94  93  92  91  90

I circled at first, then I started to swoop,
Then I flustered a farmer while looping the loop.

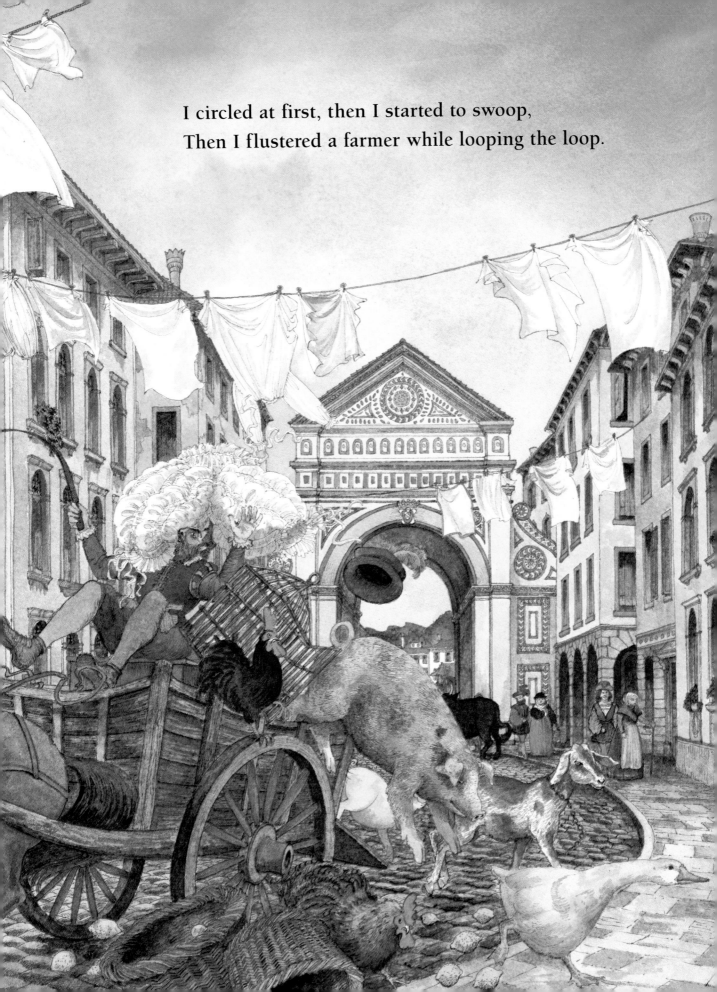

Safe by the river! But just for a minute—
A brute of a bull went and landed me in it.

I thought I was sinking, when somebody seized me.
She scrubbed me and rubbed me, then rinsed me and squeezed me.

Back on the riverbank, chilly and damp,
I was sniffed at and snatched by a mischievous scamp.

We raced 'round a corner and down to the sea,
And I started to think I would *never* be free.

Then I heard a meow and the patter of paws,
And my kidnapper growlingly opened his jaws.

I soared through the masts like a bird through the trees,
And I flew from the top like a flag in the breeze.

Buffeted back from the sea by a squall,
I was helped on my way by a blow from a ball.

Close to the castle I glided so low
That I toppled a knight as he tackled his foe.

Then just when I thought I was safe from the fray
I was caught by an arrow and carried away.

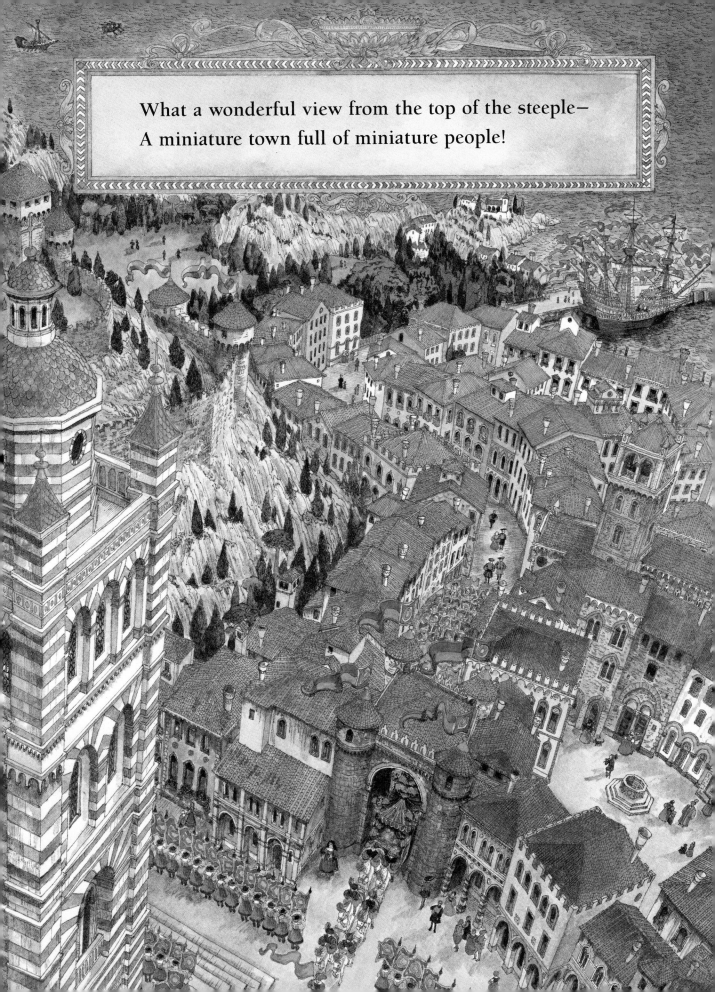

What a wonderful view from the top of the steeple—
A miniature town full of miniature people!

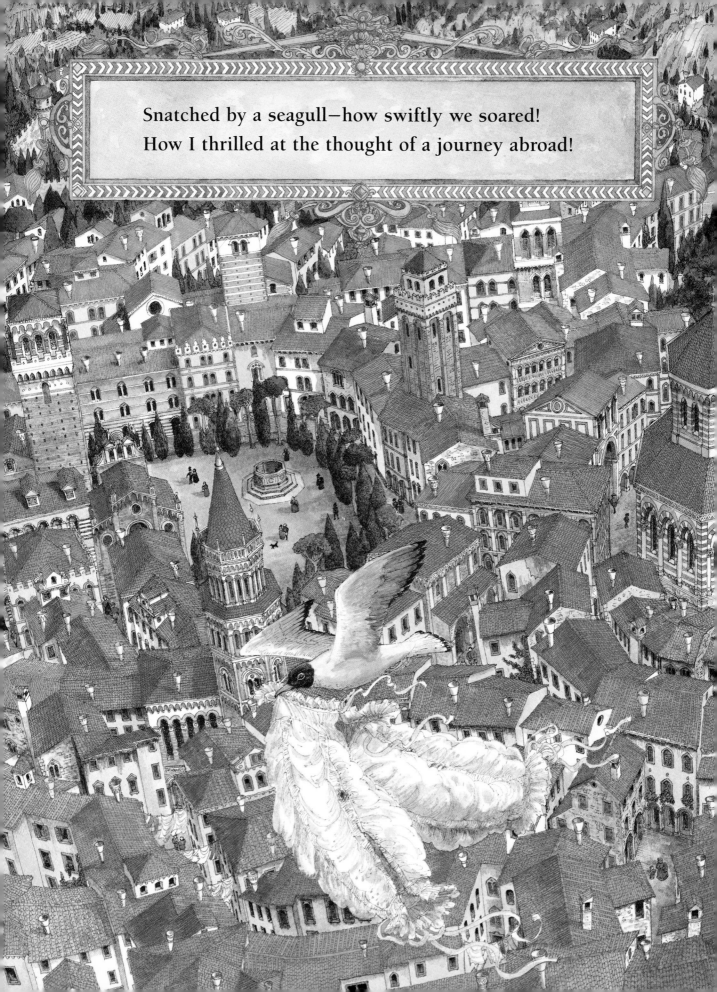

Snatched by a seagull—how swiftly we soared!
How I thrilled at the thought of a journey abroad!

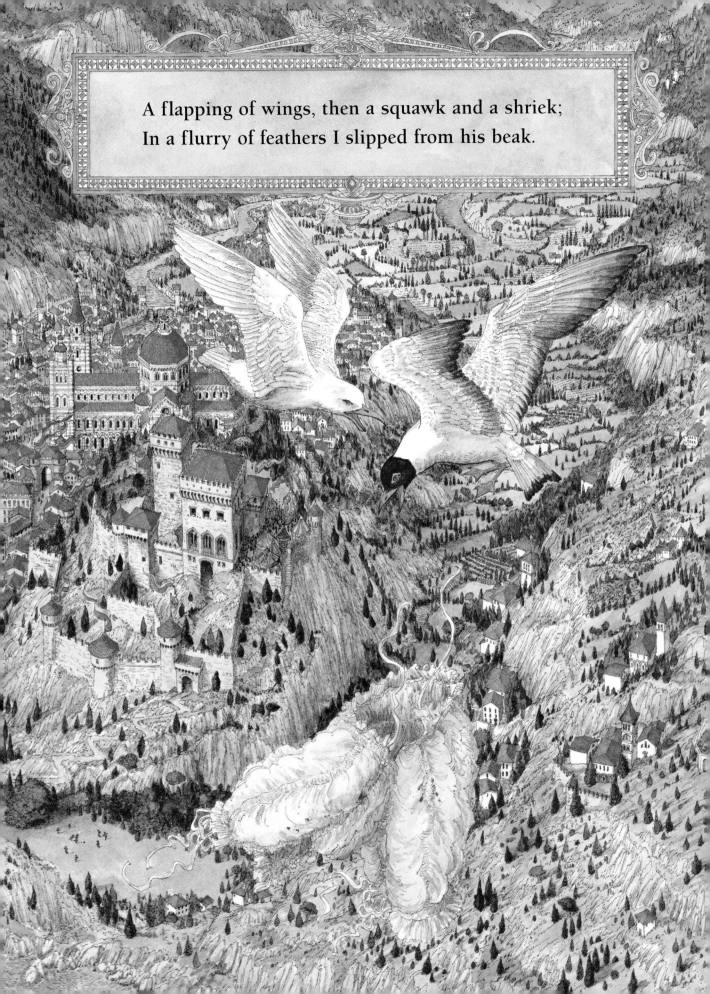

A flapping of wings, then a squawk and a shriek;
In a flurry of feathers I slipped from his beak.

The wind blew me back from the ships and the shore,
And below me were rooftops I knew from before.

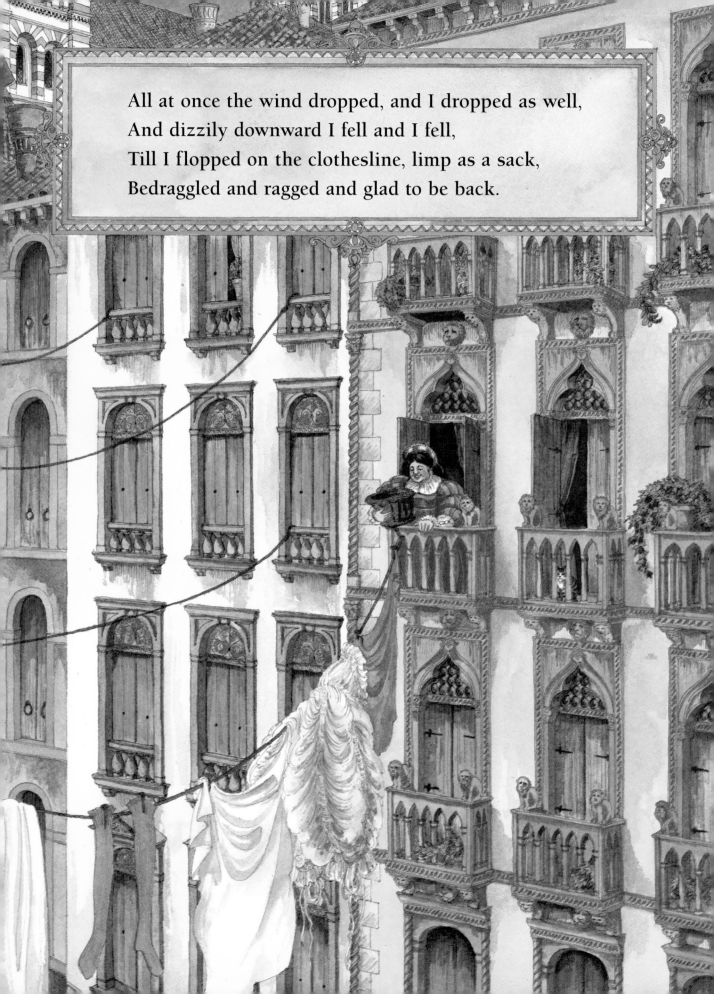

All at once the wind dropped, and I dropped as well,
And dizzily downward I fell and I fell,
Till I flopped on the clothesline, limp as a sack,
Bedraggled and ragged and glad to be back.